THERE WAS AN OLD LADY WHO SWALLOWED A FLY!

by Lucille Colandro
Illustrated by Jared Lee

Cartwheel Books
an imprint of Scholastic Inc.

With appreciation for the Cartwheel Team:
Ken, Matt, Jeff, Celia, Leslie, and Annie
—L.C.

To my wonderful wife, PJ, and
darling daughters, Jana and Jennifer
—J.L.

ISBN 978-0-545-68292-3

22 21   20 21/0

Printed in the U.S.A. 40
First printing, September 2014

There was an old lady who swallowed a fly.
I don't know why she swallowed that fly.
She won't say why.

There was an old lady who swallowed a spider
that wriggled and jiggled and tickled inside her.

She swallowed the spider to catch the fly.
I don't know why she swallowed that fly.
She won't say why.

There was an old lady who swallowed a bird.
How absurd, to swallow a bird!

She swallowed the bird to catch the spider.
She swallowed the spider to catch the fly.

I don't know why she swallowed that fly.
She won't say why.

There was an old lady who swallowed a cat.
Imagine that, she swallowed a cat.

She swallowed the cat to catch the bird.
She swallowed the bird to catch the spider.
She swallowed the spider to catch the fly.

I don't know why she swallowed that fly.
She won't say why.

There was an old lady who swallowed a dog.

What a hog! To swallow a dog!

She swallowed the dog to catch the cat.
She swallowed the cat to catch the bird.
She swallowed the bird to catch the spider.

She swallowed the spider to catch the fly.
I don't know why she swallowed that fly.
She won't say why.

There was an old lady who swallowed a goat.
Just opened her throat and swallowed a goat!

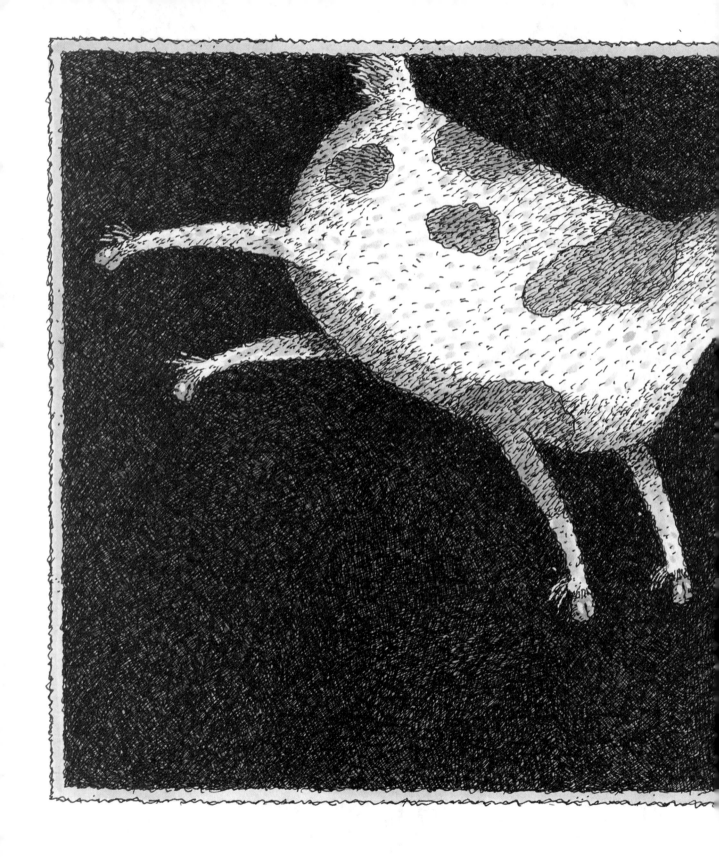

She swallowed the goat to catch the dog.

She swallowed the dog to catch the cat.

She swallowed the cat to catch the bird.

She swallowed the bird to catch the spider.

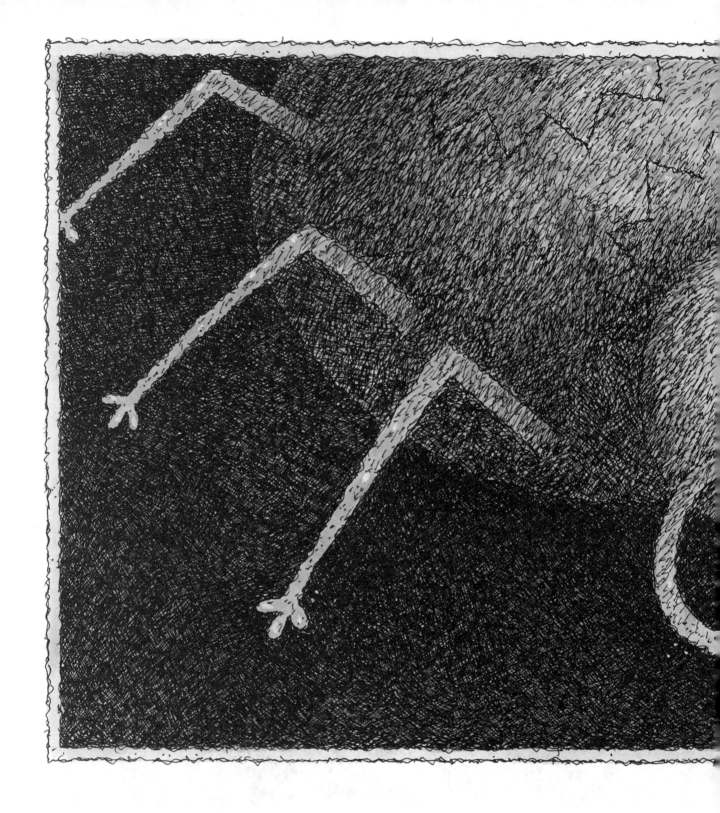

She swallowed the spider to catch the fly.

I don't know why she swallowed that fly.
She won't say why.

There was an old lady who swallowed a cow.
I don't know how she swallowed that cow.

But swallowing the animals is not how this ends, because she coughed so hard . . .

COUGH!

... out flew all her new friends!